Same Difference

by

Calida Garcia Rawles

www.samedifferencebook.com
ISBN 978-0-9856832-0-7

Second Edition

To
Chana and Summer
for brightening
the colors of my childhood
and
Skye and Sage
for creating new ones.

Lisa and Lida were
just the same.
Practically twins, even down
to their names. They were first
cousins who loved to play.
They were never apart, not
even for a day.

Lida and Lisa danced
to the same beat, sang the
same songs,

and even sat in the
same seat.

On hot days,
they swam at the pool

and walked home
together every day
after school.

When they played
they shared
imaginary friends,

hosted tea parties,
and hoped the days
would never end.

One day at their
grandmother's house,
they dressed in her beautiful
pearls and
became more than just
two pretty little girls.

In front of the mirror,
they played like
princesses.
But when they looked
closely, they just saw
differences.

Lisa said, with a big frown, "Your skin is tan, and my color is brown."

Lida said,
"Your hair
is short, and
mine is long.
One of our
hairstyles must
be wrong!"

Confused, the two girls ra[n]
straight to their grandmoth[er.]

Togethe[r]
they aske[d,]
"Why don't we loo[k]
like each other[?"]

Grandmother said
with a grin,
"To me, you look
just like twins.
You both have on pink
dresses and shoes,
and even have the same
cute hairdos."

"No, no.
That's not right," Lisa said.
"My skin is dark,
and hers is light.
And our hair,
it's different, too.
We're not the same,
no matter what we do."

"Is one better?" asked Lida. "Is one worse? If this was a contest, who would come in first?"

"Oh, children, let me explain.
You can be different and still
be the same.
No one is better.
No one is first.

You come from people who
look very diverse.
Like different times in the
same day,
both are beautiful
in their own way."

"Lida,
your skin color is
like the morning's
golden sky, with
rich vanilla creams
and honey yellow
clouds passing by.

Lisa,
your skin color has
cinnamon red hues,
mixed with
sweet purple plums
and the sky's
midnight blues."

"I know hair is special
to a little girl.
But let me tell you,
you both have the same curl,

just different sizes—
one big and one small.
Having natural beauty
is special to us all."

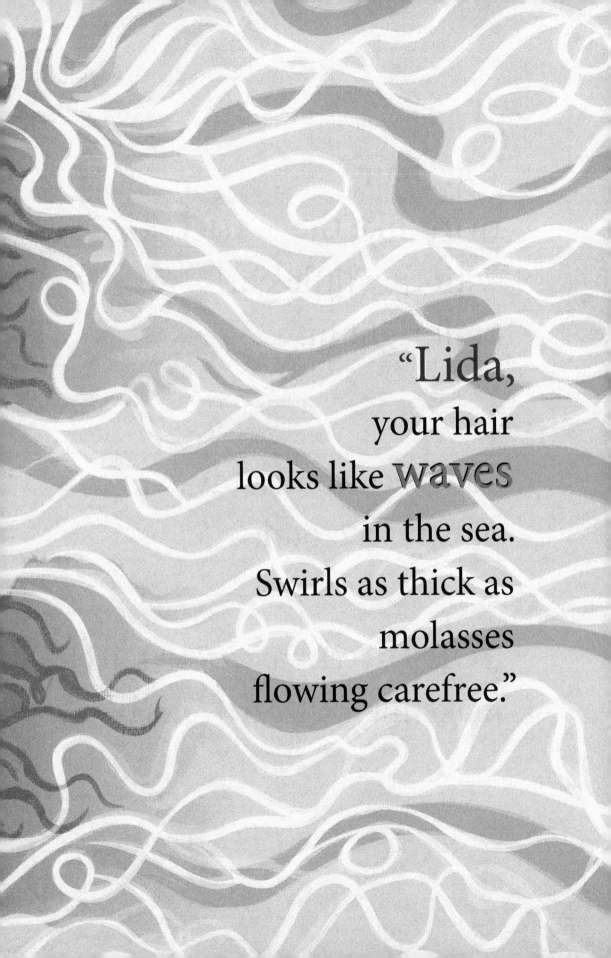

"Lida,
your hair
looks like waves
in the sea.
Swirls as thick as
molasses
flowing carefree."

"Lisa,
your hair
twirls like the wind,
with tiny little curls
built right in.

Soft as cotton candy,
puffy as a cloud.

You both have ponytails that
make me very proud."

"So now I hope you see just how **wonderful** yo **both** can be.

Light or dark skin,
short or long hair,
you're both special
because of what you share."

Lida and Lisa
decided to play in front of the
mirror for the rest of the day.

They were two happy girls,
no more, no less.
Just the same smile
in the same pink dress.

Same difference is what they
would say
if their hair or skin ever got
in their way.

They were first cousins
who loved to play.
They were   apart,
not even for a day.

CPSIA information can be obtained
at www.ICGtesting.com
Printed in the USA
LVHW060354011019
632762LV00001B/1/P